For Annie and Harriet. Always. —F.S.
For Joanne —M.B.

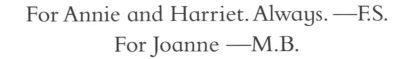

Text copyright © 2019 by Frances Stickley
Jacket art and interior illustrations copyright © 2019 by Migy Blanco

All rights reserved. Published in the United States by Random House Children's Books,
a division of Penguin Random House LLC, New York.
Originally published in hardcover by Nosy Crow Ltd, London, in 2019.

Random House and the colophon are registered
trademarks of Penguin Random House LLC.

Visit us on the Web! rhcbooks.com

Educators and librarians, for a variety of teaching tools, visit us at RHTeachersLibrarians.com

Library of Congress Cataloging-in-Publication Data is available upon request.
ISBN 978-0-593-12400-0 (trade) — ISBN 978-0-593-12558-8 (ebook)

MANUFACTURED IN CHINA
10 9 8 7 6 5 4 3 2 1
First American Edition

LOVE YOU ALWAYS

by Frances Stickley   illustrated by Migy Blanco

Random House 🏠 New York

Little Hedgie and his mommy snuffled home beneath the trees.
The leaves were rustling softly in the gentle autumn breeze.

Little Hedgie shivered as the leaves came drifting down.

"Everything feels different now,"
said Hedgie with a frown.

"Everything is changing," Mommy said. "It's nature's way.
But change makes nature lovelier with every passing day."

Hedgie looked around him, and he suddenly felt strange.
"Mommy . . .

would you love me MORE," he wondered, "if I changed?"

"Would you love me **more**
if I could dart across the leaves?
What if I were like a squirrel
dashing through the trees?"

"Imagine that," said Mommy.
"How exciting it would seem,
but I couldn't love you more
if you could race the rushing stream."

"Would you love me **more** if I could fly up in the sky?
What if I could flutter like a dainty dragonfly?"

"Imagine that," said Mommy.
"How you'd sparkle, little one,
but I couldn't love you more
if you could soar up to the sun."

"Would you love me **more** if I could leap along a log?
What if I could bounce across the lilies like a frog?"

"Imagine that," said Mommy. "What a joy to jump so high,
but I couldn't love you more if you could spring into the sky."

"Would you love me **more** if I had smooth and silky hair?
What if I were fluffy like the rabbit over there?"

"Imagine that," said Mommy.
"Fur or prickles, I'd be proud,
but I couldn't love you more
if you were softer than a cloud."

"But, Mommy," Hedgie wondered, "will love always last forever, even if I change just like the seasons or the weather?"

"ALWAYS," Mommy said.
"As long as skies are high above . . .

there's one thing that will never change,"
she promised. . . .

"And that's love."

"I'll love you always, little one. I've loved you from the start.
I'll tell you every day, until you know the words by heart."

"Always," whispered Hedgie
as he curled up in his bed.
"Imagine that . . . ," he murmured.

"Just imagine," Mommy said.